Pokémon

TOTODILE IN LOVE

A Valentine's
Day Sticker
Storybook

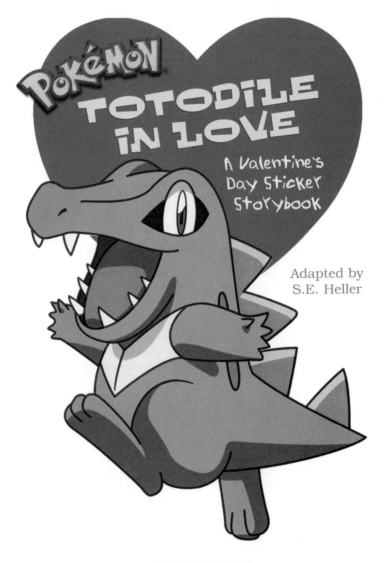

POKÉMON
TOTODILE IN LOVE

A Valentine's Day Sticker Storybook

Adapted by
S.E. Heller

SCHOLASTIC INC.

New York   Toronto   London   Auckland   Sydney

Mexico City   New Delhi   Hong Kong   Buenos Aires

ISBN 0-439-35804-3

12 11 10 9 8 7 6 5 4 3 2   2 3 4 5 6 7/0

Printed in the U.S.A.
First Scholastic printing, January 2002

Chapter 1

A LOVELY LAKE

It was a beautiful day. Ash Ketchum and his friends, Misty and Brock, had been traveling together for a long time. The Pokémon trainers were ready for a break. They stopped near a big, blue lake.

Pikachu, Ash's Electric Pokémon,

and Togepi, Misty's little Pokémon, were glad to have a rest. Pikachu had been by Ash's side through all his travels. And Misty took special care of little Togepi.

"*Brrr*," squealed Togepi. *This lake looks like fun!*

Misty agreed. She called her

Water Pokémon to come out and play.

First there was  .

Goldeen looked like a fancy goldfish. Staryu was next. It was a Star Shape Pokémon. Then came Poliwhirl, which had a round body with swirls. They were all happy to be in the water together.

"Pokémon need to have fun just as much as their trainers do," said Brock.

"*Pika*," Pikachu agreed. *We sure do!*

Ash remembered that he had a Water Pokémon, too.

"Come out, Totodile!" Ash called.

A little blue Pokémon popped out of its Poké Ball. It looked like a blue crocodile. It was .

"*Totodile!*" it shouted when it saw the lake. *Hooray!*

Totodile jumped into the water. Then it saw three Magikarp swimming nearby. They were orange Fish Pokémon. Totodile opened its mouth and made a water fountain.

It juggled the Magikarp in the moving water.

"Totodile is really talented," said Misty.

"*Pika*," Pikachu agreed. Totodile loves to show off!

Chapter 2
LOVE AT FIRST SIGHT

Totodile floated on its back. It tapped its belly. *Rum, pum, pum.* Totodile was making music.

But Totodile could hear another kind of music, too. The Water Pokémon liked the sweet sound. It peeked over some rocks. There was a Pokémon singing in the water. It was  .

Totodile thought Azumarill was the most beautiful Pokémon in the world. It was blue, with long ears and spots on its belly. Bubbles floated around it like magic.

"Totodile!" Totodile raced over the rocks to Azumarill. *Here I come!*

The beautiful Pokémon stopped singing.

"Azumarill!" Azumarill said.

Leave me alone.

But Totodile was in love! It made a water fountain in the shape of a heart.

Azumarill did not like the heart. It wanted Totodile to stop. Azumarill sprayed Totodile with a Water Gun Attack. Totodile fell backward, but it did not give up. It began to chase after Azumarill.

Chapter 3

LOVE IN THE AFTERNOON

"There you are!" said a pretty girl named Beverly.

Azumarill ran to her trainer. Beverly had been looking for her missing Azumarill all day. Two Pokémon were helping. They were  and  .

Pikachu and Ash were happy, too. The friends had never seen an Azumarill before.

Ash's Pokémon computer, Pokédex, said that Azumarill was an Aquarabbit Pokémon. It could use its long ears to hear sounds that were far away, even underwater.

Right now, Azumarill's ears were turned toward the trees. It looked nervous.

"What is wrong, Azumarill?" Beverly asked.

Just then, Totodile ran into the

clearing. It crashed to the ground in front of Azumarril.

"Hey! What are you doing, Totodile?" asked Ash.

Totodile lifted its head. Heart-shaped bubbles floated out of its mouth.

"Azumarill!" shouted Azumarill. *Stop that! You are embarrassing me.*

Azumarill blushed and hid behind Beverly. The Aquarabbit Pokémon was mad at Totodile for embarrassing it.

Chapter 4

SHOWING OFF

Beverly told the friends that she and her Pokémon were in a traveling circus.

"Pika," said Pikachu. *Wow!* Being in a circus sounded like fun.

"But there have been problems with Azumarill." Beverly sighed. "Ever since Golduck joined us,

Azumarill's been acting strangely. She used to love performing. But now she skips practices. We spend a lot of time looking for her."

Just then, Brock and Totodile rushed by. They were going to help set up the stage for the circus. Brock wanted to impress Beverly. Totodile wanted to impress Azumarill. They were both acting a little goofy.

Totodile filled a pool with water. It picked up Azumarill and carried it to the pool.

Azumarill did not like being treated this way. It blasted Totodile with water again.

Chapter 5
CIRCUS SURPRISE

Finally, it was time for the circus. Beverly started with a magic act. Marill, a blue Mouse Pokémon, jumped into her hat. Beverly tapped the hat three times. A flock of Pidgeys flew out. Then Beverly put the hat on her head. When she pulled it off, there was .

"Beverly is amazing," said Misty.

"She sure is." Brock sighed. He always fell for pretty girls. Now it was time for the star of the show. Azumarill created fountains of water and made colorful balls dance on top. The crowd was thrilled, especially Totodile. It jumped out of Ash's arms and ran onstage.

Totodile made a fountain like Azumarill. The crowd laughed. They threw fruit for Totodile to juggle. The audience loved seeing the two Pokémon performing together.

But Azumarill did not want to share the spotlight. Azumarill stopped its water fountain. The colorful balls fell to the ground.

"Azu azu!" Azumarill was mad.

"Quit it, Totodile!" yelled Ash. He and Pikachu tried to stop Totodile, but it was too late. Azumarill was running off the stage. Totodile followed.

Suddenly, all of the fruit began to fall. Ash caught bananas and oranges. stood on Ash's head. The little yellow Pokémon caught the last apple.

22

"Hooray!" yelled the crowd. They thought Ash and Pikachu were part of the show.

Chapter 6
TEAM ROCKET TROUBLE

Someone was watching from backstage. It was Team Rocket. The two teenagers and their talking Pokémon, Meowth, were trouble-makers. They were always trying to steal Pokémon. The leader of the group was Jessie. Today she had one of her meanest plans ever.

"If we kidnap Azumarill and Pikachu, we can start our own traveling circus!" she said.

 and James thought this

was a great idea. They wanted to be rich.

As Team Rocket prepared its evil plan, Brock was giving Totodile lessons in love. Totodile wanted to learn how to win Azumarill's heart. Brock said to do it with presents.

Totodile took a special jar of Pokémon food to Azumarill. But the beautiful Pokémon was still mad at Totodile. It did not want the present. This made Totodile sad.

"Do not give up!" Brock encouraged Ash's Pokémon.

Totodile chased Azumarill. Then, suddenly, a net fell from the sky. It dropped on Azumarill.

Totodile was shocked! It tried to grab the net, but it was too slow.

Azumarill was lifted into a hot air balloon.

Team Rocket laughed. Jessie's plan was working.

Chapter 7
A CAGE FOR PIKACHU

Ash and Misty came running to help. They were angry when they saw that Team Rocket had stolen Azumarill.

"How about using Thunderbolt?" Ash asked Pikachu.

"Pika," Pikachu nodded. It was ready to blast Team Rocket.

But that was just what Meowth
was hoping for. When Pikachu
jumped in the air, Meowth
dropped a cage on top of the
Electric Pokémon. The cage
snapped shut around Pikachu.

"Pickachuuu!" The little Pokémon sparked lightning. But the Thunderbolt Attack could not get through the cage. Team Rocket just laughed.

James threw a Poké Ball and called for  .

"Weezing, use Smoke Screen!" ordered James.

Black smoke filled the air. Ash, Misty, and Brock could not see a thing. And the smoke made them cough. Only Totodile was able to escape from Weezing's attack.

Totodile watched Team Rocket float over the lake. A pink bow fell from Azumarill's tail. Totodile caught it. *My poor Azumarill,* thought Totodile, *and my friend, Pikachu.* Totodile was determined to save the Pokémon from Team Rocket.

"Totodile!" it cried. *I will not give up!*

With that, Totodile jumped into the lake and began to swim after the hot air balloon.

"Come back Totodile!" Ash cried.

But Totodile was determined to help Azumarill and Pikachu.

Chapter 8

TOTODILE IS TRAPPED

Azumarill would not perform for Jessie. It was making Jessie mad.

"I have an idea," said James. "If we treat our star right, then Azumarill will do what we want."

James offered Azumarill balls to juggle. They fell to the ground. He prepared a great feast. Azumarill would not eat a thing.

"Being nice does not work," said Jessie. "It is more fun to be nasty."

But Totodile had finally caught up to Team Rocket. It leaped up

and knocked Jessie and James to the ground with a powerful Water Gun Attack.

"Pika!" Pikachu cheered for its friend. Even Azumarill was happy to see Totodile.

"Not so fast!" cried Meowth. The talking Pokémon threw a lasso around Totodile. Totodile was trapped! Its mouth was tied tight. Totodile could not spray water anymore.

Team Rocket cheered. "Now we can have a *three*-ring circus," Meowth said, smiling.

Chapter 9

FRIENDS AT LAST

That night, Azumarill was sad. Totodile wanted to cheer it up. The crocodile Pokémon gave Azumarill its pink bow through the cage bars.

"Azumarill." Azumarill smiled. *Thank you.*

Totodile was glad to see Azumarill smile. It began to jump

up and down, waving its arms and legs.

Azumarill thought that Totodile was funny. Soon all of the Pokémon were smiling. It was good to be with friends.

Chapter 10
RESCUE

The next morning, Jessie put the Pokémon cages in the hot air balloon. Team Rocket had a new plan: They were going to bring Azumarill, Pikachu, and Totodile to their boss, Giovanni.

"Giovanni will pay us well for three rare Pokémon," said Jessie.

James turned on the hot air. But as the balloon started to lift off, Beverly's Pidgey flew by. Pidgey tore a hole in the balloon with its beak.

Whoosh! Team Rocket was grounded. The Pokémon cages

tumbled to the ground.

"Pikachu!" Ash cried happily, catching the cage that held his Pokémon.

"Totodile!" shouted Brock. Totodile's cage rolled right into his arms.

Poor Azumarill! Her cage did not roll off the balloon. Team Rocket grabbed the circus star.

"We will never hand over this Azumarill!" said Meowth.

Beverly, Ash, Misty, and Brock did not agree.

Beverly grabbed a Poké Ball. "Go

get her, Golduck!"

James called Weezing. Jessie called Arbok, a Snake Pokémon. But Team Rocket's Pokémon did not stand a chance. Golduck blasted Weezing and Arbok with a powerful stream of water.

Then Ash took out a Poké Ball. He called , a Plant Pokémon.

Bulbasaur used a Razor Leaf Attack to cut through the bars of the cages. Pikachu and Totodile were free!

"Use Water Gun," Ash told Totodile.

With great aim, Totodile sprayed Jessie, James, and Meowth. Team Rocket fell backward.

Now Bulbasaur grabbed Azumarill's cage with its strong vines. Bulbasaur pulled Azumarill to safety.

"Thunderbolt, Pikachu!" cried Ash.

The little yellow Pokémon was ready.

"Pikachuuu!" The powerful attack sent Team Rocket blasting

through the air. They disappeared
with a *ping*.

Chapter 11
A PERFECT MATCH

Bulbasaur used its Razor Leaf Attack to set Azumarill free.

"*Zoo, zoo.*" Azumarill smiled happily.

Totodile and Golduck watched Azumarill run toward them.

"You have won the battle of love," Brock told Totodile. He

smiled at the Pokémon. "Go to Azumarill!"

Totodile ran to Azumarill. It felt like a dream. Azumarill smiled happily. Totodile smiled happily.

But Azumarill ran right past Totodile.

"Huh?" The friends stared in surprise. Azumarill ran straight

into Golduck's arms.

Golduck hugged Azumarill. They were in love.

"Pika?" Pikachu asked. *What happened?*

"Azumarill has been lovesick for Golduck," said Beverly. "That explains why it has been acting so strangely."

"Poor Totodile!" said Misty.

But Totodile did not stay sad for long. There was a beautiful Pokémon down by the lake. It was a Quagsire wearing a lovely red bow.

"*Totodile!*" Totodile went running to meet it.

"Oh, great!" said Misty. "A Pokémon that acts just like Brock!"

As the friends ran after Totodile, Brock offered some advice. "When it comes to love, never give up!"